DAVID GETS HIS DRUM

David "Panama" Francis
and Bob Reiser

Illustrated by Eric Velasquez

Marshall Cavendish • New York

I am a drummer man. They call me "Panama" because when I play the drums I always wear a white Panama hat. For seventy years I have beat out that dancing sound for millions of people, from Japan to France to the USA. Every time I see folks smile and tap their feet to the rhythm, I feel as happy as I did on the day that I first beat a pair of sticks on an old tin can.

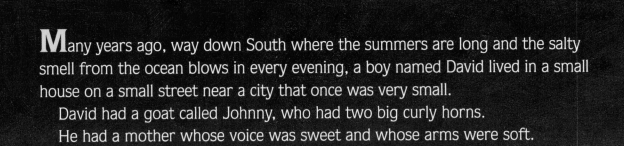

Many years ago, way down South where the summers are long and the salty smell from the ocean blows in every evening, a boy named David lived in a small house on a small street near a city that once was very small.

David had a goat called Johnny, who had two big curly horns.

He had a mother whose voice was sweet and whose arms were soft.

Text copyright © 2002 by David Panama Francis and Bob Reiser.
Illustrations copyright © 2002 by Eric Velasquez.
All rights reserved
Marshall Cavendish, 99 White Plains Road, Tarrytown, NY 10591

Library of Congress Cataloging-in-Publication Data
Francis, David.
David gets his drum / David (Panama) Francis and Bob Reiser.
Illustrated by Eric Velasquez.
p. cm. Summary: In this story based on the life of drummer
David "Panama" Francis, a little boy named David dreams of getting
his own drum and marching in the Sunday parade.
ISBN—0-7614-5088-2 1. Francis, David (Panama)—Childhood and
youth—Juvenile fiction. [1. Francis, David (Panama—Childhood and youth—
Fiction. 2. Musicians—Fiction. 3. Drum—Fiction.] I. Reiser, Bob. II. Title
PZ7.F8469 Dav 2001 [E]—dc21 00-047425

The text of this book is set in 13 point Quorum Book.
The illustrations are rendered in oils on paper.
Printed in Malaysia.
First edition
6 5 4 3 2 1

His dad came from Haiti. And when he mixed a pot of tearfully hot Haiti chicken, he told stories about that green island and its magical drums. When his dad spoke in that deep island voice, David could almost hear the magic drums in his head.

On Saturday nights when his dad and mom
cooked together, the house was set for a feast.
They would pile the table with Dad's chicken
and Mom's cool conch fritters from the Island
of Nassau, where she was born. David loved
family meals!

After dinner came music. Up on a table stood
a record player, one that you had to wind up first.
His dad even got a special stool so David could
climb up and wind the player himself.

Out of those spinning black records came the sound of the bands playing. They played slow marches and fast marches and sad marches and happy jumping music that made you want to dance.

David closed his eyes and there he was, marching down the street, playing the drums, leading the band, dressed in pure white so the sun made him shine.

David was a drummer. He felt it with the itch in his fingers and the rhythm in his wrists. He was a drummer just like "Brulla" Roberts.

Every Sunday, "Brulla" Roberts led the St. Agnes band right down 15th Street. Brulla and his shining snare drum, keeping the beat, all the trombones and trumpets and clarinets following close behind.

Rum-tum-tum-pet-y-tum-tum-tum

Down the muddy streets they came,

Ta-ran-ta-ta Ta-ran-ta-ta

People and dogs and chickens ran from their houses to listen.

Tweety tweet tweety tweet

Every Sunday was a holiday in old Miami.

While Mom and Dad were washing the dishes,
David marched around the house like Brulla.
He tried keeping time with spoons, knives—even
his shoes—but nothing sounded like Brulla's magic drum.
Once he even tried taking apart a kitchen chair to make
drumsticks. But Mom only got mad and made him spend
all night gluing the chair back together.

One Sunday morning David opened his eyes and saw something on the foot of his bed. It was a package wrapped in brown paper. He tore off the paper, and his eyes popped open. It was a real drum with real sticks, and it was little, just the right size for a six-year-old boy! Now he could drum like Brulla!

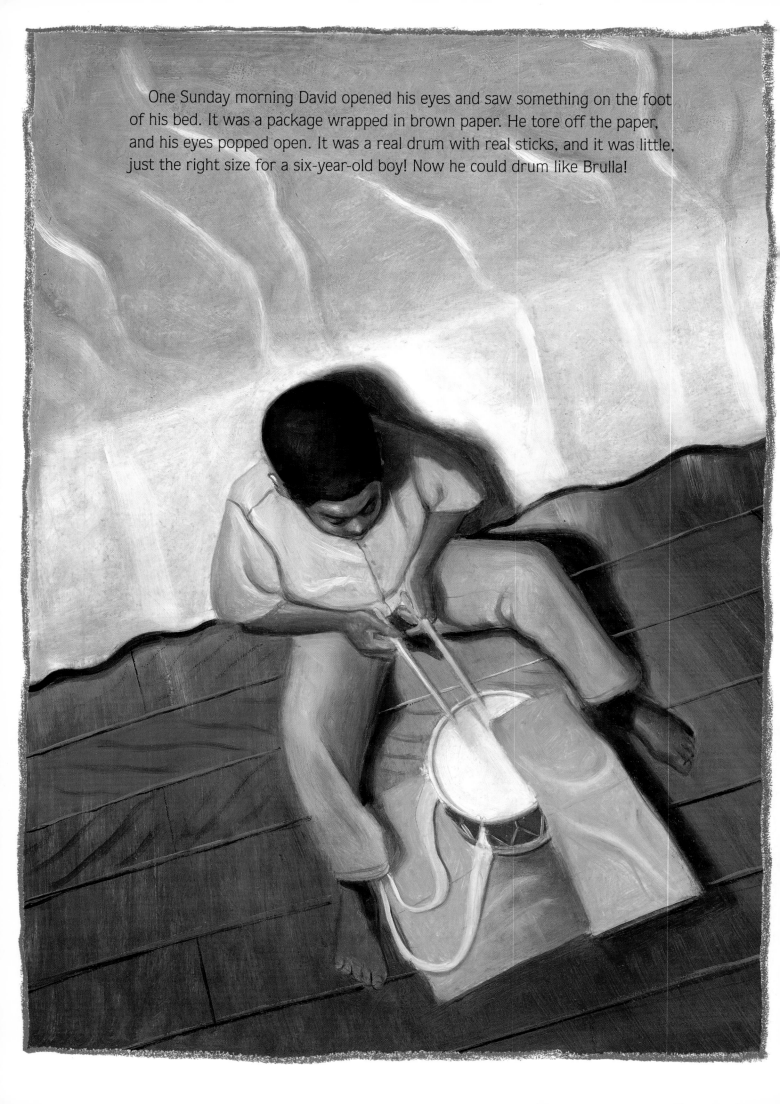

He pulled on his clothes and ran out of his room. Mom and Dad were waiting for him. "If you love to drum, then you should drum," said his dad. "Now you don't have to break the furniture."

David was so happy he hugged his dad, kissed his mom and his sister Iona, grabbed his real sticks and his real drum, and ran outside.

He beat the drum for Johnny the Goat and for Papa Charlie the junk man!

Rat tat tat!

Tat-tat-ley tat tat tat.

Tat-tat-ley tat tat tat.

He beat that rhythm that made you dance!

Tat-tat-ley tat tat tat!

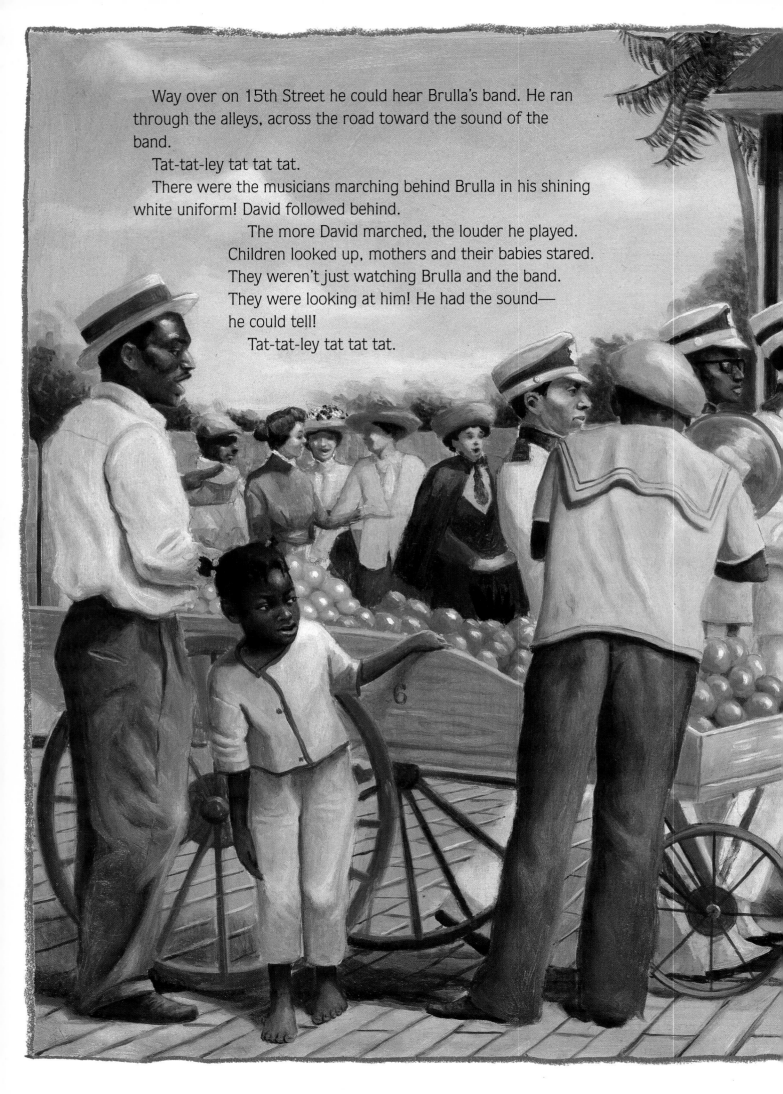

Way over on 15th Street he could hear Brulla's band. He ran through the alleys, across the road toward the sound of the band.

Tat-tat-ley tat tat tat.

There were the musicians marching behind Brulla in his shining white uniform! David followed behind.

The more David marched, the louder he played. Children looked up, mothers and their babies stared. They weren't just watching Brulla and the band. They were looking at him! He had the sound— he could tell!

Tat-tat-ley tat tat tat.

He was in the middle of them now, walking right behind the trombones. He swung his arms high in the sky just like Brulla. Suddenly,

Tat-tat-ley tat tat splat!!!
A terrible sound came out of the drum. David hit it again.
Thump thump ey thump thump thump
He looked down at his drum and his heart dropped. The top
of the drum was torn wide open.
Everybody was looking at him—he couldn't let them see him cry.
So, he wiped his eyes and slowly walked home, tapping softly on his
broken drum.
Thump . . . thump . . . ey . . thump thump thump.
He walked slower and slower toward his house.

Then, as he passed Papa Charlie's junkyard, he saw an old oatmeal box. It was round and almost as wide as his drum! He yanked the round top off the box, flattened it out by spreading out its sides. It just fit over the drum. He banged it.

Thump . . . Off it popped.

Then he saw some old nails lying on the ground. Carefully he sat down in front of his house with the boxtop, the nails, and a big stone. He took off the old drumtop. Wham wham wham! Now the oatmeal boxtop couldn't come off!

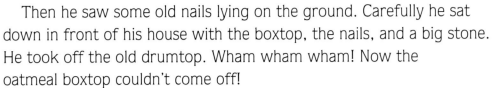

He raised his drumsticks—bonk bonk braaaak! He looked down. His stick had gone right through the boxtop! He was too strong!

His eyes started to sting again.

"David . . ." he heard his mom call.

He could smell Sunday dinner cooking, but he had to fix his drum! He looked around the yard. There! Johnny the Goat was chewing on a big old peaches can.

Quietly he crept up behind Johnny. He reached out and grabbed the can. Johnny tugged on it. David tugged. Johnny tugged. David tugged and he got it!

Quick as the wind, David ran into the house.

The house smelled of fried chicken. His Mom and his Dad and Iona were all sitting down to eat. He was so hungry. But he had to fix his drum.

"David!" his dad sounded worried. "Are you all right?"

David ran into his room and closed the door before they could see the broken drum.

"David!" his mom shouted.

"I'll eat later!" David answered, and he got to work. He took the top of the peaches can and, being careful not to cut himself, he glued it on top of the torn boxtop. It still had Johnny's teeth marks. He raised his stick and—tong a tong tong. It didn't sound like a real drum at all!

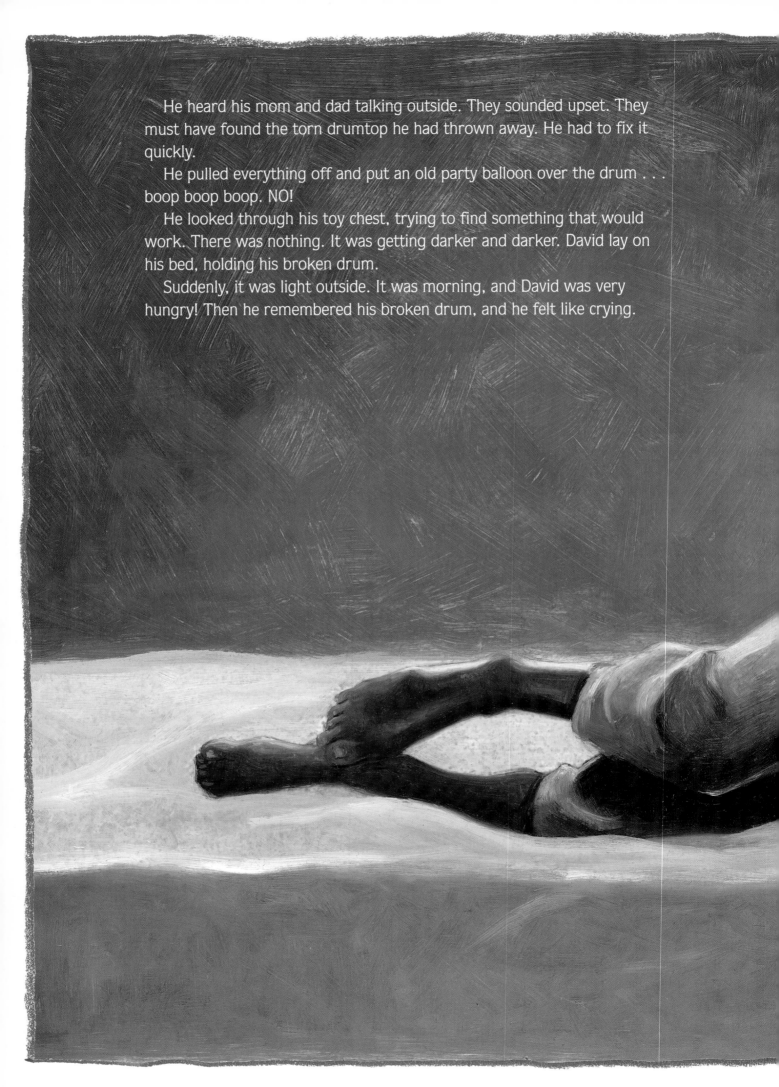

He heard his mom and dad talking outside. They sounded upset. They must have found the torn drumtop he had thrown away. He had to fix it quickly.

He pulled everything off and put an old party balloon over the drum . . . boop boop boop. NO!

He looked through his toy chest, trying to find something that would work. There was nothing. It was getting darker and darker. David lay on his bed, holding his broken drum.

Suddenly, it was light outside. It was morning, and David was very hungry! Then he remembered his broken drum, and he felt like crying.

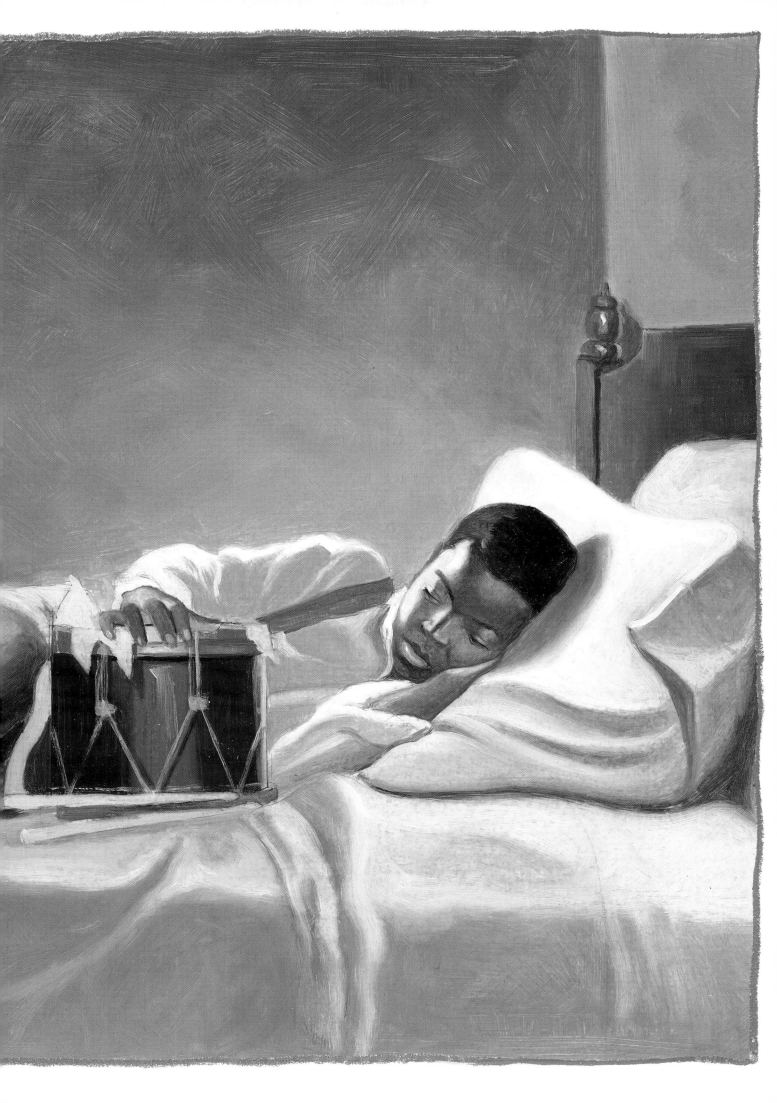

He knew his mom and dad were probably upset, but he picked up his drum, and opened his door. His mouth dropped open in surprise.

Sitting at the breakfast table with his mom, dad and sister was a big man with a snow-white suit. The man turned to David. "I hear you like to drum!" His voice had the deep music of the Islands, just like his dad's.

David nodded and grabbed a biscuit. The man looked very familiar, maybe because he came from the Island of Haiti, just like Dad.

"I like drums, too," smiled the man. "Can I see yours?"

David gasped. The man was Brulla Roberts! "I . . I . . . " David stammered. He couldn't let Brulla see his broken drum.

"Please," said Brulla.

Slowly David held out his drum with papers and balloons and nails sticking out of it. It looked even worse than he remembered.

"Hmmm . . . " Brulla looked at him. "It's hard to make music on a drum like that."

David nodded.

"He's too strong for a little drum," said his mom.

Brulla looked at him for a long time. "He must like to drum very very much." David's face turned red. He bet Brulla had never broken his own drum.

"Maybe he needs a drum like this . . ." Brulla reached under the table and brought out the most amazing drum David had ever seen. It looked just like Brulla's silver-and-white drum, but it was smaller, and the top was made out of metal. David stared at it. It looked beautiful . . . "This was my first drum," explained Brulla Roberts.

David reached out his hand. Then he stopped. "Can I touch it?"

Brulla nodded. David's hand touched the smooth shiny metal around the rim. Brulla watched him very seriously.

"Put the cord around your neck," Brulla said softly. David slipped the smooth rope around his neck. The drum hung in front of him. Brulla put two drumsticks into David's hands. David knew just how to hold them.

David looked up at Brulla to ask if he could play.
Brulla nodded.

Te ter tum . . terum rum tum a tum a tum
atummey tum te tum . . . The sound
pinged off the strong steel top and
bounced through the air.
Rum atum te te te tum te te tum!

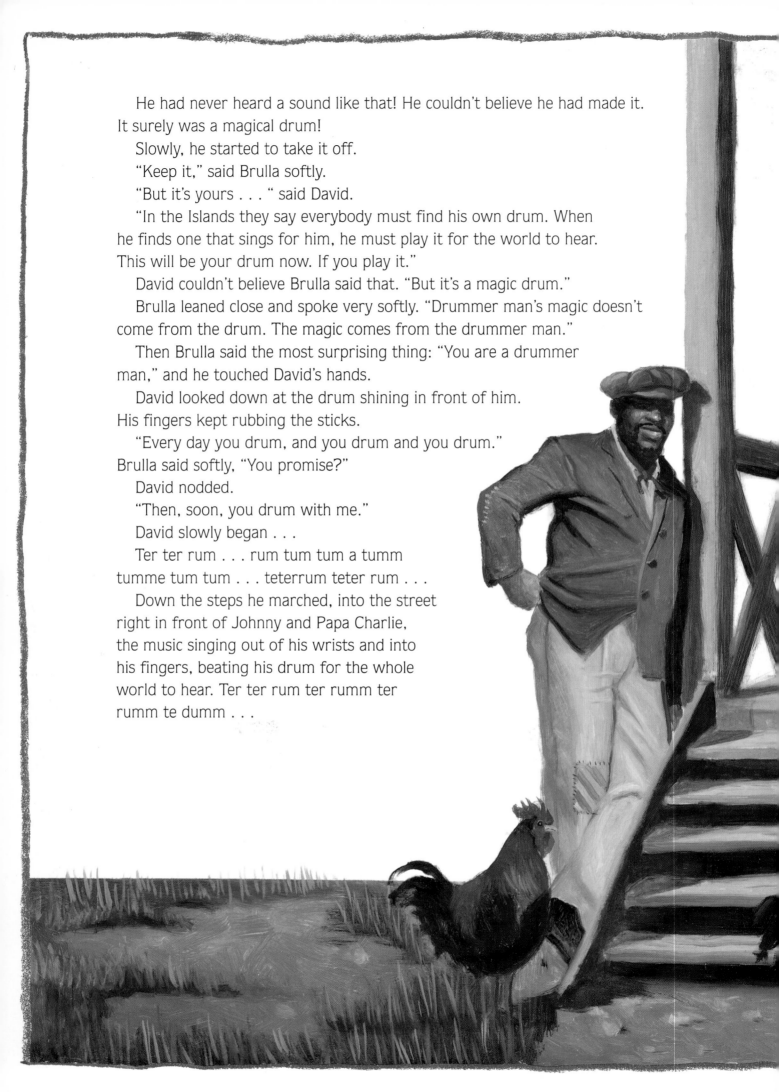

He had never heard a sound like that! He couldn't believe he had made it.
It surely was a magical drum!

Slowly, he started to take it off.

"Keep it," said Brulla softly.

"But it's yours . . . " said David.

"In the Islands they say everybody must find his own drum. When
he finds one that sings for him, he must play it for the world to hear.
This will be your drum now. If you play it."

David couldn't believe Brulla said that. "But it's a magic drum."

Brulla leaned close and spoke very softly. "Drummer man's magic doesn't
come from the drum. The magic comes from the drummer man."

Then Brulla said the most surprising thing: "You are a drummer
man," and he touched David's hands.

David looked down at the drum shining in front of him.
His fingers kept rubbing the sticks.

"Every day you drum, and you drum and you drum."
Brulla said softly, "You promise?"

David nodded.

"Then, soon, you drum with me."

David slowly began . . .

Ter ter rum . . . rum tum tum a tumm
tumme tum tum . . . teterrum teter rum . . .

Down the steps he marched, into the street
right in front of Johnny and Papa Charlie,
the music singing out of his wrists and into
his fingers, beating his drum for the whole
world to hear. Ter ter rum ter rumm ter
rumm te dumm . . .

Afterword

I was little David Francis. Today they call me Panama. I did get to play in the marching band.

I grew up and left Miami and Brulla Roberts to play drums in New York. I got to play for some of the world's greatest band leaders, and made hundreds of records heard by people around the world. Now I live in Florida. But every chance I get, I am out playing that rum-tum-tum-ter-tum-te-tum-tum rhythm that makes you want to dance. I will never stop being a drummer man.